Six S*****r
Easy-to-Read
Stories

BARNES
&NOBLE
BOOKS
NEW YORK

Scholastic Inc.

To Jordan
— G.M.

For my dentist,
Dr. Dan Epstein
— B.L.

My Tooth Is About to Fall Out! (0-590-48376-5)
Text copyright © 1995 by Grace Maccarone.
Illustrations copyright © 1995 by Betsy Lewin.

Soccer Game! (0-590-48369-2)
Text copyright © 1994 by Grace Maccarone.
Illustrations copyright © 1994 by Meredith Johnson.

The Classroom Pet (0-590-26264-5)
Text copyright © 1995 by Grace Maccarone.
Illustrations copyright © 1995 by Betsy Lewin.

Mr. Rover Takes Over (0-439-20057-1)
Text copyright © 2000 by Grace Maccarone.
Illustrations copyright © 2000 by Meredith Johnson.

Pizza Party! (0-590-47563-0)
Text copyright © 1994 by Grace Maccarone.
Illustrations copyright © 1994 by Emily Arnold McCully.

"What Is That?" Said the Cat (0-590-25945-8)
Text copyright © 1995 by Grace Maccarone.
Illustrations copyright © 1995 by Jeffrey Scherer.

Club compilation ISBN: 0-439-54255-3

10 9 8 7 6 5 4 3 2 1   03 04 05 06 07

Printed in Singapore 46 • This edition first printing, March 2003

This edition created specially for Barnes & Noble, Inc.
0-7607-4096-8

My Tooth Is About to Fall Out

by Grace Maccarone
Illustrated by Betsy Lewin

Hello Reader! — Level 1

SCHOLASTIC INC.

Uh-oh!
It wobbles.
It wiggles.
It joggles.
It jiggles.
My tooth
is about
to fall out.

I hope it doesn't fall
while I am playing ball

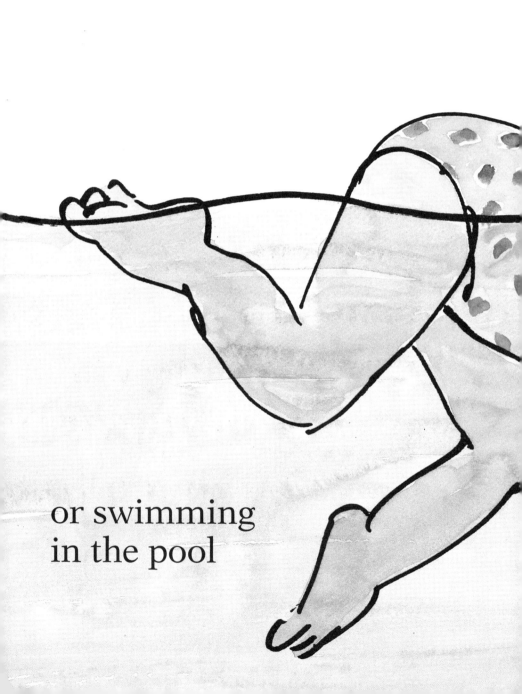

or swimming
in the pool

or having
fun at school.
But most of all,

I hope it doesn't fall
into my meatball
or in my spaghetti.

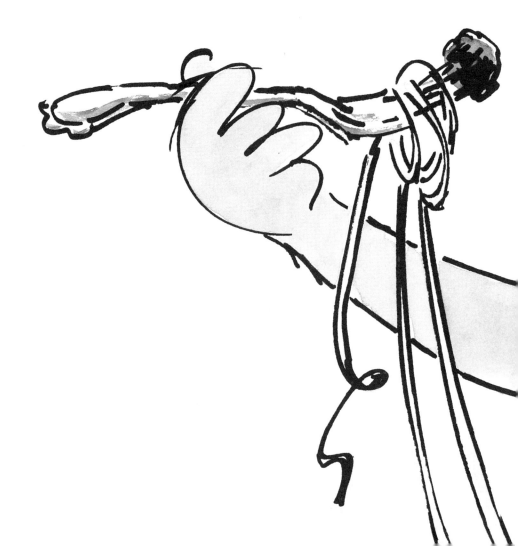

Oops!
It's already
gone!

My tooth is
in my bowl.

My tongue
can feel the hole.

It feels funny.
Nothing's there.
My tongue slides through.
There's only air.

Now that space
gives my face
a brand-new,
big-kid smile.

Then tonight I'll
go to sleep.
And the Tooth Fairy
will creep
into my room.

She'll take my baby tooth,
and maybe,
if I'm lucky,
she will leave
something behind
for me to find.

I had twenty
baby teeth —
with big ones
growing underneath.

My roots, I think,
dissolve and shrink
until they're small.
And so my teeth
get loose and fall.

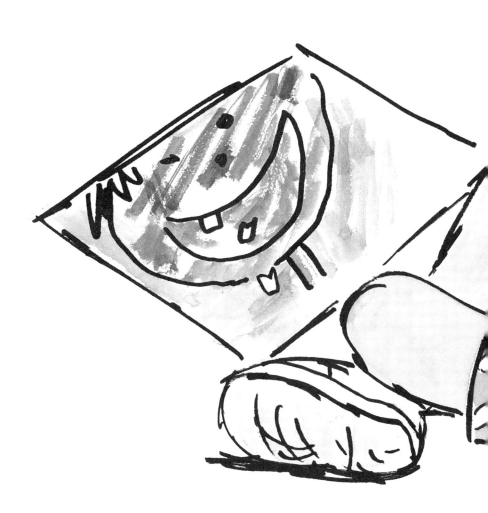

My big teeth will
begin to show
from under my gums,
way below.

I can't wait
to see them.
They'll look
great!

SOCCER GAME!

To Rachel and Joey
— G.M.

SOCCER GAME!

by Grace Maccarone
Illustrated by Meredith Johnson

Hello Reader! — Level 1

SCHOLASTIC INC.

We start the game.

We're ready.

We aim.

We pass.

We fall.

They get the ball.

Away they go!

We're doomed!
Oh, no!

It's in the air.

Our goalie is there!

We dribble.

We pass.

We slip
on the grass.

We kick. We run.

We're having fun!

We see a hole.

We run to the goal.

The ball goes in.

Hooray! We win!

The
Classroom Pet

To Betsy Lewin
        — G. M.

To Seraphina Dilcher
        — B. L.

The Classroom Pet

by Grace Maccarone
Illustrated by Betsy Lewin

Hello Reader! — Level 1

SCHOLASTIC INC.

It's the day
before Christmas ...
It's almost three.
The class is sitting quietly
to hear who gets
the classroom pets.

The snake goes home with Kim.

The rabbit goes with Dan.

The ant farm goes with Max.

The hamster goes with Jan.

Sam gets the crab.
Her name is Star.

Oops! Star falls down in Mommy's car.

Sam gives Star water.
Sam gives Star bread.

Sam says good night
and goes to bed.

Sam wakes up
to something great.
Star is eating
from her plate.

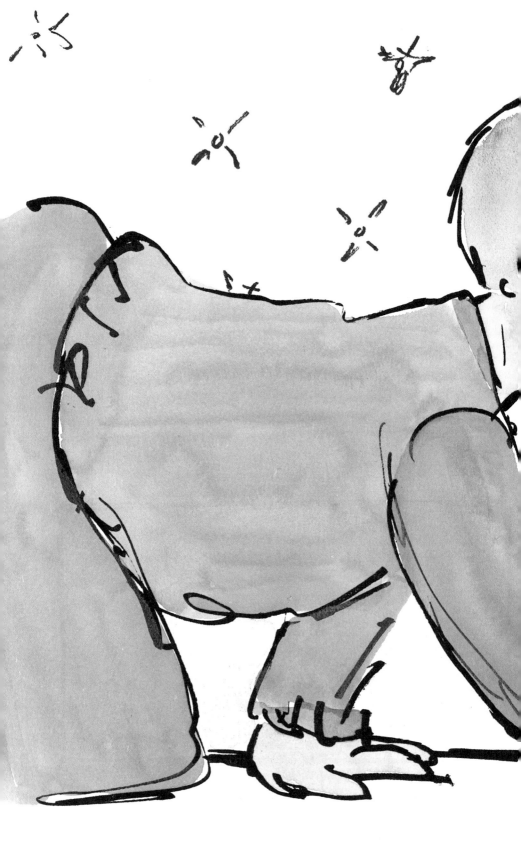

In the kitchen,
Sam lets Star crawl
across the floor,
along the wall.

Sam turns around
to get a pear.
When Sam turns back,
Star is *not* there!

Where is Star?
Where did she go?
Sam looks high.

Sam looks low —

under the bed,

under a chair,

with the toys.

No! Not in there!

Sam wants to cry.
Where could Star be?
Now Sam sees
the Christmas tree!

Then Sam takes back
the classroom pet.
And this is a story
that Sam won't forget.

Mr. Rover Takes Over

To Ryan with love
—Aunt Gracie

For Amanda Paxton
—M.J.

Mr. Rover Takes Over

by Grace Maccarone
Illustrated by Meredith Johnson

Hello Reader! — Level 1

SCHOLASTIC INC.

"Mrs. Katz is sick,"
our principal said.

"You will have a new teacher just for today."

"Boo!" said the class.

We did not want a new teacher.
We wanted Mrs. Katz.

"You will like him,"
the principal said.
"His name is Rover—Mr. Rover."

Our class was surprised
that the teacher was a man.

But we were wrong.

Our new teacher was a dog.

It started out as a normal day.

We had spelling.

We had math.

Recess was fun.
Mr. Rover played catch with us.

He played tag with us.

He even played
basketball with us.

Mr. Rover barked to let us know
that recess was over.

Some kids kept playing anyway.

Mr. Rover nipped their ankles.
He herded them into the
classroom.

But something bad
had happened.

Our class pet, Mousy,
was not in his cage!

"He is lost," said Penny.
"He will die," said Ben.

Some kids cried.

Mr. Rover barked.

He put his nose to the ground.

We put our noses to the ground.

He crawled out the door.

We crawled out the door.

He sniffed.

We sniffed.

We found Mousy!

Our class had fun when
Mr. Rover took over.

But we were happy when
Mrs. Katz came back.

Pizza Party!

*To three men who love to cook
with kids: Nick Keyembe,
David Heckerling, and Salvatore Maccarone
—G.M.*

Pizza Party!

by Grace Maccarone

Illustrated by Emily Arnold McCully

Hello Reader! — Level 1

SCHOLASTIC INC.

We scoop.
We pour.

We pour some more.

We fill.
We spill.

We wipe the floor.

We clean.

We fix.

We help to mix.

We push.

We poke.

We roll.

We joke.

We wait awhile.

We play.

We smile.

We pull.

We toss.

We stretch,

add sauce.

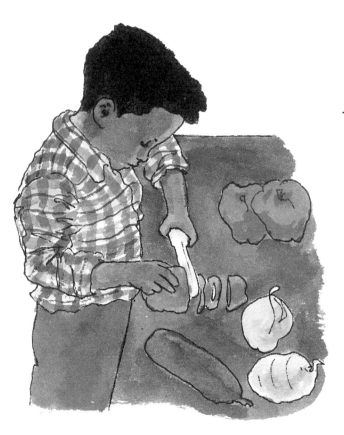

We cut.

We shred.

We taste.

We spread.

It cooks.
We look.

We read a book.

It's done.
What fun!

We eat our pie.

We're done!
What fun!

We say good-bye!

"What Is THAT?" Said the Cat

To Edie,
who always makes me look good!
— G.M.

For Ruth,
the greatest storyteller of them all
—J.S.

"What Is THAT?" Said the Cat

by Grace Maccarone
Illustrated by Jeffrey Scherer

Hello Reader! — Level 1

SCHOLASTIC INC.

"I found a box," said the fox.

"I heard," said the bird.

"What is that?"
said the cat.

"We don't know," said the crow.

"It is big," said the pig.
"Let me see," said the bee.

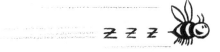 

"Open it up," said the pup.
"How?" said the cow.

"I'll use force,"
said the horse.

"Use a bat," said the rat.
"I will try," said the fly.

"Good luck," said the duck.
"Beware!" said the hare.

CLICK

Then

the fox

and the bird

and the cat

and the crow

and the pig

and the bee

and the pup

and the cow

and the horse

and the rat

and the fly

and the duck

and the hare

said,

"See you later,

alligator!"